"HELLO READING books are a perfect introduction to reading. Brief sentences full of word repetition and full-color pictures stress visual clues to help a child take the first important steps toward reading. Mastering these storybooks will build children's reading confidence and give them the enthusiasm to stand on their own in the world of words."

—Bee Cullinan
Past President of the International Reading
Association, Professor in New York University's
Early Childhood and Elementary Education Program

"Readers aren't born, they're made. Desire is planted—planted by parents who work at it."

—Jim Trelease
author of *The Read-Aloud Handbook*

"When I was a classroom reading teacher, I recognized the importance of good stories in making children understand that reading is more than just recognizing words. I saw that children who have ready access to storybooks get excited about reading. They also make noticeably greater gains in reading comprehension. The development of the HELLO READING stories grows out of this experience."

—Harriet Ziefert
M.A.T., New York University School of Education
Author, Language Arts Module,
Scholastic Early Childhood Program

For Camp Greylock

PUFFIN BOOKS
Published by the Penguin Group
Viking Penguin, a division of Penguin Books USA Inc.,
40 West 23rd Street, New York, New York 10010, U.S.A.
Penguin Books Ltd, 27 Wrights Lane, London W8 5TZ, England
Penguin Books Australia Ltd, Ringwood, Victoria, Australia
Penguin Books Canada Ltd, 2801 John Street, Markham, Ontario, Canada L3R 1B4
Penguin Books (N.Z.) Ltd, 182–190 Wairau Road, Auckland 10, New Zealand

Penguin Books Ltd, Registered Offices: Harmondsworth, Middlesex, England

Published in Puffin Books, 1990

1 3 5 7 9 10 8 6 4 2
Text copyright © James Ziefert, 1990
Illustrations copyright © Mavis Smith, 1990
All rights reserved

Library of Congress Catalog Card Number: 89-62905
ISBN: 0-14-054223-X

Printed in Singapore for Harriet Ziefert, Inc.

Harry Goes To Day Camp

James Ziefert
Pictures by Mavis Smith

PUFFIN BOOKS

"The bus is here!
The bus is here!"
said Harry's mother.

Harry took his camp bag.
He took his lunch bag.
And he ran out the door.

Harry got on the bus.
He found a good seat.
He was off to camp!

Everybody on the bus sang:
99 bottles of beer on the wall
99 bottles of beer
If one of the bottles should happen to fall…

98 bottles of beer on the wall
98 bottles of beer...
If one of the bottles
should happen to fall...

97 bottles of beer on the wall
96 bottles...95 bottles...
94 bottles...93 bottles...
92 bottles...91 bottles...

"We're at camp!"
said the bus counselor.
"Everybody off!
And take your stuff!"

Harry found his group.
He found his counselor.

He gave his lunch
to his counselor.

He put his bag
in his cubby.

"What do we play first?"
Harry asked.
"Soccer," said the counselor.

"Aww! Soccer!" Harry whined.
"When do we go swimming?"
"Later," said the counselor.

Harry played soccer.

Harry played...

but not very well!

"What do we play next?"
Harry asked.
"Basketball," said the counselor.

"Aww! Basketball!" Harry whined.
"When do we go swimming?"
"Later," said the counselor.

Harry played basketball.

Harry played...

but not very well!

It was time for lunch.
Harry liked lunch.
He ate everything.
And he drank his milk.

"When do we go swimming?"
  Harry asked.
"Later," said the counselor.
"After lunch we rest."

Harry rested.
He rested on his mat.
He rested until he heard,
"It's time for swimming!"

"Hey! Hey!" Harry yelled.
"Let's go!"

Harry was the first one ready.

Harry jumped into the pool.
He made a big splash!

Harry was a great swimmer.

He swam with his head
out of the water.

He swam with his head
in the water.

He floated on top of the water.

He paddled under the water.

And he raced!

"Harry is the winner!"
yelled the counselor.
"Hooray for him!
Everybody out of the water!"

Harry's counselor said,
"It's time for music."

"Aww!" said Harry.
"When do we go swimming?"